SNO-ISLE REGIONAL LIBRARY

☞ W9-CAY-147

998

WITHDRAWN
Sno-Isle Libraries

Copyright © 1998 by Anita Jeram

All rights reserved.

First U.S. edition 1998

Library of Congress Cataloging-in-Publication Data

Jeram, Anita.
Birthday happy, Contrary Mary / Anita Jeram. — 1st U.S. ed.
p.   cm.
Summary: When the little mouse, Contrary Mary, appears to be unhappy at her most
unusual birthday party, her father knows just what to do to get her to laugh.
ISBN 0-7636-0448-8 (hardcover) — ISBN 0-7636-0456-9 (paperback)
[1. Mice — Fiction. 2. Birthdays — Fiction. 3. Parties — Fiction. 4. Behavior — Fiction.] I. Title.
PZ7.J467Bi   1998
[E] — dc21   97-20615

2 4 6 8 10 9 7 5 3 1

Printed in Singapore

This book was typeset in Columbus MT.
The pictures were done in watercolor and ink.

Candlewick Press
2067 Massachusetts Avenue
Cambridge, Massachusetts 02140

Birthday Happy, Contrary Mary

Anita Jeram

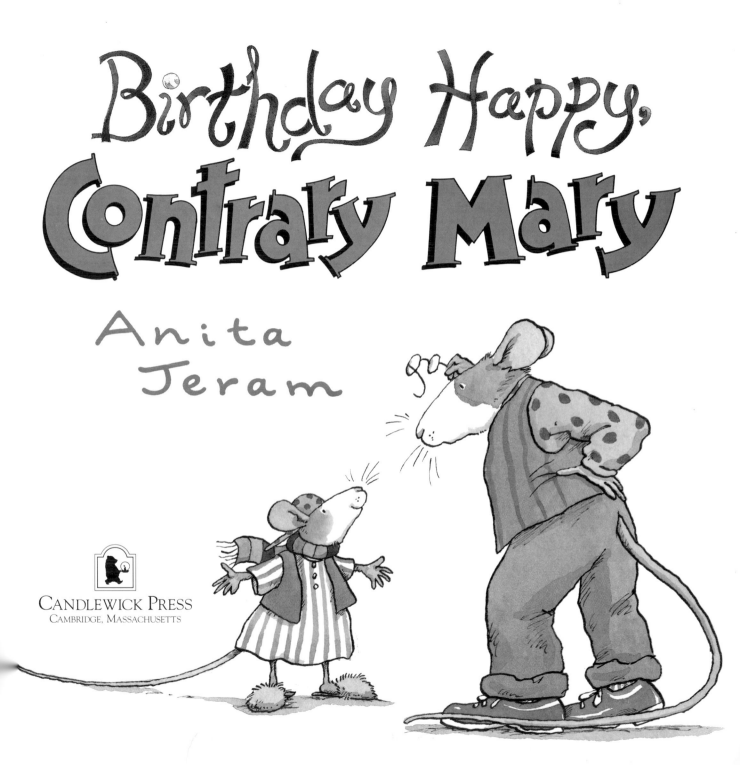

CANDLEWICK PRESS
CAMBRIDGE, MASSACHUSETTS

Today was Contrary Mary's birthday. "Happy birthday!" said her mom and dad. "Happy every day," said Contrary Mary. She loved the presents her mom and dad gave her.

"Much you very thank!" she said.

Mary tried out her new stilts—upside down. Then she piled her new farm animals into her new polka-dot cap and said, "This box makes a good hat."

After breakfast Mary
helped her mom
make things for
her birthday party.
She made inside-out Swiss
cheese sandwiches
and frosted all
the cupcakes
upside down.

Then she went
upstairs to put
on her party
clothes.

"Come in," Mary's dad said to her friends when they arrived for the party. "We're playing hide-and-seek." It wasn't hard to find Mary. They played hide-and-seek again and again, and Mary was always the first one found.

When they
played music
and everyone
was dancing,
Contrary Mary
sat on the floor.

Then, when the music
stopped and everyone
flopped to the floor,
Contrary Mary
danced.

At lunchtime, everyone loved the inside-out sandwiches and got frosting on their chins eating the cupcakes. Contrary Mary ate her Jell-O with a knife and fork, and everyone copied her.

 Mary's mom brought out
her birthday cake.
"Happy birthday to you!"
everyone sang.
But Contrary Mary
did not look
happy,
not
one
bit.

Then Contrary Mary's
dad had an idea.

He sang,
"*You to birthday happy*
You to birthday happy
Mary Contrary, birthday happy
You to birthday happy!"
Contrary Mary laughed
and blew out her candles
and everyone shouted,

"Birthday happy,
Contrary Mary!"